The Better-Than-Best Purim

written and illustrated by

Naomi Howland

Text and illustrations copyright © 2012 by Naomi Howland
All rights reserved
Amazon Publishing
Attn: Amazon Children's Books
P.O. Box 400818
Las Vegas, NV, 89140
www.amazon.com/amazonchildrenspublishing

The illustrations are rendered in gouache and colored pencil.
Book design by Vera Soki
Editor: Margery Cuyler

Printed in Malaysia   2019
021423K2
022030.5K4/B571/A3

Library of Congress Cataloging-in-Publication Data
Howland, Naomi.
The better-than-best Purim / written and illustrated by Naomi
Howland. — 1st ed.
p. cm.
Summary: To celebrate Purim an old woman makes
hamantaschen cookies, with no assistance from her lazy pets
who are secretly planning a surprise. Includes author's note on
the origin of this festive holiday and a recipe for hamantaschen.
ISBN 9781477847671 (paperback) —
ISBN 978-0-7614-6204-0 (ebook)
[1. Purim—Fiction. 2. Baking—Fiction. 3. Cookies—Fiction.
4. Pets—Fiction. 5. Old age—Fiction.] I. Title.
PZ7.H847Be 2012   [E]—dc23   2011049503

For Susannah & Justin
and
Juliet & Kelly

"Purim is coming! Time to bake some better-than-best hamantaschen," said the little old lady. "Will you help me?" she asked her cross-eyed cat.

The cat stretched and said, "Is Purim so soon?"
"Very soon!" said the little old lady.

"Uhmm, I'm too busy right now," said the cat. "I have to wash my fur." And she jumped off the chair.

The little old lady turned to her noisy parrot. "Will you help me make some better-than-best hamantaschen?"

The parrot stopped preening his feathers and said, "Is it really almost Purim?"

"Almost," said the little old lady.

"Maybe later," squawked the parrot. "I'm going to play pirates. Arrgh!" And he flew out of the kitchen.

The little old lady woke her one-spotted dog. "Can you help me make some hamantaschen? The cat is washing her fur, and the parrot is playing pirates."

The dog yawned and said, "Sorry, I can't. I'm going to catch a ball." He trotted out of the room.

"Those animals are no help at all," huffed the little old lady. "I will have to make some better-than-best hamantaschen all by myself!"

So she measured and sifted and sifted and measured.

Then she scooped and mixed and mixed and scooped. She beat the butter and broke the eggs and grated and added a teaspoon of her secret special ingredient.

Crash!
Bang!

"What's going on in there?" called the little old lady.

"Nothing," answered the animals.

"Good! Then you can help me roll out the dough for better-than-best hamantaschen," replied the little old lady.

"I'm cleaning my whiskers," said the cat.

"I want a cracker," sang the parrot.

"I'm chasing my tail," said the dog.

"There's always an excuse!" complained the little old lady.

And she floured and rolled and rolled and floured and cut out little circles.

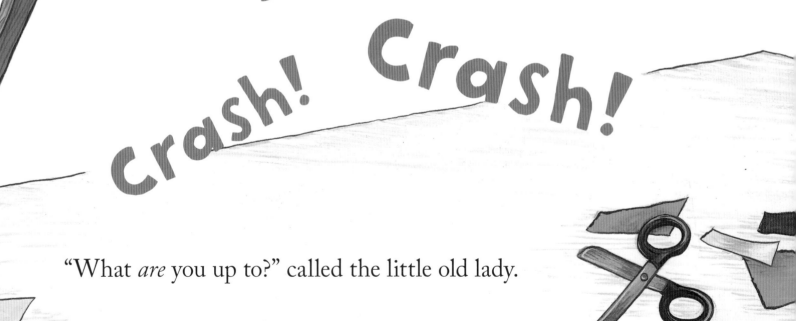

Bang!

Crash! Crash!

"What *are* you up to?" called the little old lady.

"Nothing!" answered the animals.

"Fine!" exclaimed the little old lady. "Then you can help me fill this dough for better-than-best hamantaschen."

"I'm taking a nap," said the cat.

"I'm flying to Peru," shouted the parrot.

"I'm fetching a stick," said the dog.

"Hummph! They never want to work!" grumbled the
little old lady. "I'll have to fill the hamantaschen myself."
And she folded and pinched and pinched and folded
until she had dozens of perfect triangles.

She put the trays in the oven and waited
for the hamantaschen to bake.

The dog sniffed the air. "We'd better hurry," he said.

Soon the little old lady took the trays—
one, two, three, four—out of the oven.
"I can't eat all these myself," she said. "Who will
help me eat my better-than-best hamantaschen?"

"I will," said the cross-eyed cat.

"I will," screeched the noisy parrot.

"Me too!" said the one-spotted dog.

"I don't know if I should share any of my better-than-best hamantaschen." The little old lady pouted. "You didn't help make them."

"But we were busy!" said the animals all together.

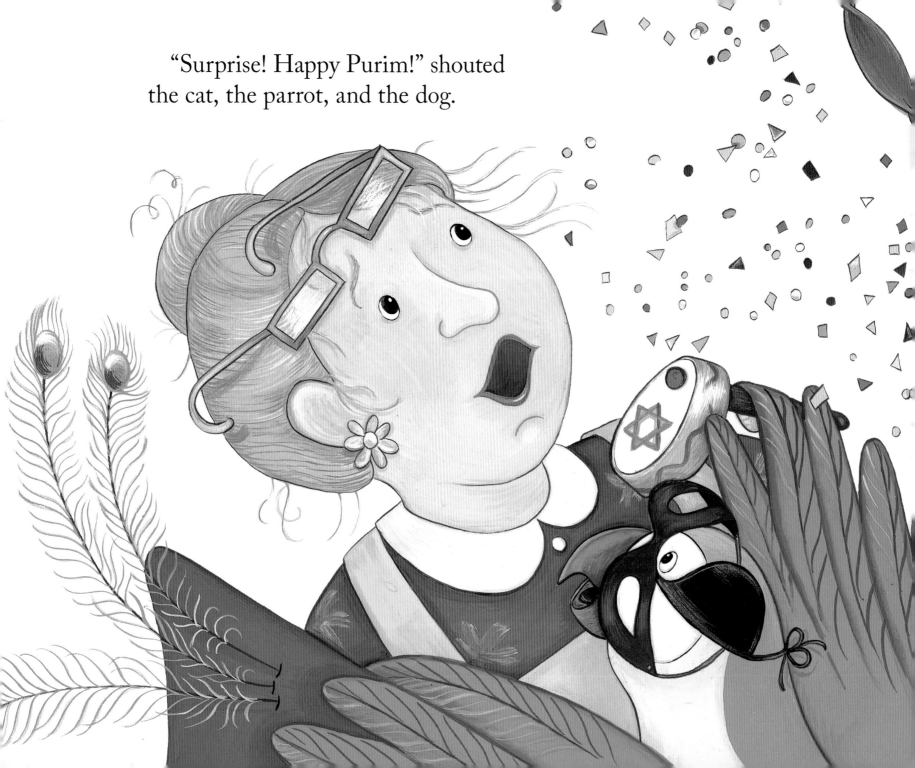

"Surprise! Happy Purim!" shouted the cat, the parrot, and the dog.

There were masks and streamers, music and noisemakers. And there were baskets of goodies for all their friends.

The little old lady and her friends danced
and sang, told stories, and played games.

They ate dozens of hamantaschen and had the better-than-best Purim party ever.

And everyone helped clean up.

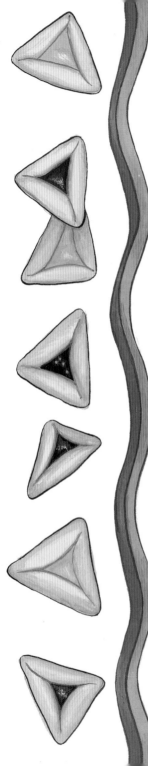

Better-Than-Best Hamantaschen

Before you begin to cook, ask an adult for help.

1 cup unsalted butter
1 cup sugar
1 cup brown sugar
2 eggs
4 tablespoons milk
4 cups flour
4 teaspoons baking powder
2 teaspoons vanilla
rind of one orange, grated
poppy-seed paste, apricot jam, or raspberry jam for filling

1. With an electric mixer, beat butter, sugar, and brown sugar together until the mixture is light and fluffy.

2. Beat eggs, milk, flour, baking powder, vanilla, and orange rind into the butter and sugar mixture.

3. Wrap the dough in waxed paper and chill in the refrigerator for 2 hours.

4. Preheat the oven to 350 degrees.

5. Divide the dough in two. Return half the dough to the refrigerator, wrapped in waxed paper. Roll out the remaining dough about 1/8-inch thick on a floured surface with a floured rolling pin. Dust the dough with more flour as needed to keep it from sticking to the rolling pin.

6. Flour the edge of a 2 1/2- or 3-inch round cookie cutter or the open end of a glass, and cut out circles of dough. Gather the scraps and re-roll them to cut out more circles.

7. Drop 1/2 teaspoon of filling onto each circle of dough. Brush a little water around the edges of the dough. Fold the edges over on three sides to form a triangle, keeping the filling inside. Gently pinch the corners.

8. Cover a baking sheet with parchment paper. Place the hamantaschen on the baking sheet, leaving an inch or so between them.

9. Bake for 15 minutes or until the edges are golden brown. Remove from the oven and place on a cooling rack until the hamantaschen have cooled.

Makes approximately 6 dozen hamantaschen. This recipe can be cut in half.